DRONE ACADEMY

OPERATION STARGAZER

MATTHEW K. MANNING

STONE ARCH BOOKS
a capstone imprint

Drone Academy is published by Stone Arch Books,
a Capstone imprint
1710 Roe Crest Drive
North Mankato, Minnesota 56003
www.mycapstone.com

Library of Congress Cataloging-in-Publication Data is
available on the Library of Congress website.

ISBN: 978-1-4965-6076-6 (library hardcover)
ISBN: 978-1-4965-6080-3 (eBook pdf)

Summary: While Howard To has always been on the
geeky side, there's one girl who brings him out of his shell.
Unfortunately, she's Hollywood's hottest sci-fi star and about
as likely to cross Howard's path as he is likely to be struck by
lightning. But when the starlet is hounded by a stalker who
uses a drone to spy on her private life, Howard employs his
own drone to engage in aerial combat with the stalker's UAV.

Designer: Aruna Rangarajan
Production Specialist: Katy LaVigne

Elements: Shutterstock: Reinke Fox, (drones) design element
throughout, Rost9, (hexagon) Cover, design element,
Supphachai Salaeman, (graphic) Cover, design element
throughout, TRONIN ANDREI, (drones) design element
throughout, WindVector, (video) design element, cover

Printed and bound in Canada.
010790S18

TABLE OF

CONTENTS

Name: Howard To

Age: 16

Ethnicity: Vietnamese-American

Home base: Los Angeles, California

Interests: Science fiction, comic books, and all things fantasy — everything from movies starring trolls and elves to role-playing games featuring wizards and warlocks

INVISIBLE MODE ···· XXXX-XXXXX-XX-XXX-X

Drone: Redbird — the sleekest
and flashiest of all the SWARM
drones; a slick, red hot rod with
four black helicopter blades, shiny
red paint, red and yellow painted
flames on the sides, and a small
black camera in its center

90%
LOADING

90%

90%

THE SWARM

Society for
Web-Operated
Aerial
Robotic
Missions

Zor_elle

Name: Zora Michaels

Age: 16

Ethnicity: African-American

Home base: Rural Indiana

Interests: As far as her classmates know, fashion, trends, and the coolest clothes and accessories; in reality, science, computers, comic books, and SWARM; all things pink

Drone: The Beast — the largest drone on the SWARM team; several feet wide with four industrial gray helicopter blades and a black, crane-like camera; camouflage colors help it blend into its surroundings

TEAM

ParkourSisters

Name: Parker Reading

Age: 16

Ethnicity: Caucasian

Home base: New York, New York

Interests: Athletics, specifically wrestling and martial arts; computer hacking — and using her computer skills for the good of SWARM

Drone: Hacker — a small gray drone, almost bug-like in appearance; Hacker has red and green lights and six helicopter blades; the most technologically advanced drone in SWARM's arsenal

saiguy

Name: Sai Patel

Age: 15

Ethnicity: Indian-American

Home base: Savannah, Georgia

Interests: SWARM logo design, a founding member of SWARM

Drone: Solo — the smallest of the SWARM drones; bright white with four blades; a guard bar around the drone's exterior protects those blades while a harness in the center carries Sai's smartphone

CHAPTER 1

THE MAN IN THE DARK CAR

The Man in Black was listening to classical music. It always soothed him on days like today. Los Angeles traffic was never easy, and rush hour was quickly approaching. The roads were far from clear, so the Man in Black enjoyed the symphony from the cool interior of his vehicle.

His car was black. His suit was black. His sunglasses were as dark black as they came. Even his hair was black, slicked back on his head. It was a stark contrast to his complexion. But the Man in Black liked contrast. He liked his life in black and white, even if he operated in a world full of grays.

The Man in Black smiled a bright white smile. He had perfect teeth. He prided himself on his dental hygiene. He had spent a small fortune on whitening, crowns, and mouth guards over the years, but he had a million-dollar smile to show for it. He used that grin whenever possible. Now he was using it because he'd discovered a parking spot, right there across from the hotel. It couldn't be more perfect.

He parallel parked his jet-black sedan and stepped out of the car, looking from right to left, then from left to right. A crowd was forming outside the hotel, but no one had noticed him. To them, the Man in Black was nothing special. That was how he preferred things. He wasn't in the market for witnesses, after all.

The Man in Black pressed a button on his keychain, and the trunk of his dark car popped open. He walked to the back of the sedan and removed a single item from its trunk. The thing in his hands was as black as his suit. It was as sleek as his hair. It was fairly small, despite its powerful motor, and had four small blades, one mounted on each corner.

He placed the device on the sidewalk near the car and got back inside behind the wheel. He shut his door, then reached over and opened the glove box. Inside was a black remote, complete with two joysticks, a few buttons, and a small monitor. He pressed the center button, and the controller vibrated to life in his hands.

Outside the car, the small object began to hum quietly. Then it lifted up into the air, propelled by four rapidly spinning miniature blades. The dark drone rose up into the sky.

The Man in Black sank into his seat. He moved the controls with his long, rough thumbs. He smiled his bright smile, even though no one could see him. This time, the smile wasn't for them. It was for him alone.

CHAPTER 2

SNACK, INTERRUPTED

"I'm going to need you to explain this," Howard To's father said, placing the note on the kitchen table.

Howard took a bite of his cereal, trying his best to avoid eye contact with his dad. He knew what it was. He'd played hooky from school — again — two weeks ago. He was surprised it had taken so long for his parents to be notified.

"Howard," his dad said. It was one word, but somehow it was also a complete sentence.

"Sorry, Pop," Howard said. "I just . . . couldn't do it."

"You've been missing too much school," said his dad. He sat down in the empty wooden chair next to Howard. "We need to talk about this. If you're being bullied —"

"Dad!" Howard said, mortified even though they were the only two people in the kitchen. "I'm not being bullied. I haven't had a bully since, like, the first grade."

Feeling his dad's gaze on him, Howard shifted in his seat. He was uncomfortable in his academy-issued uniform — a navy polo shirt and slacks. Everyone at his private school wore the same thing, but for some reason, Howard appeared more grown up than his peers. He had been told he had "old eyes" — whatever that meant.

"Then what is it?" Dad asked. He scratched the top of his head, his fingers finding their way through his thinning black hair.

That simple act annoyed Howard. But then again, nearly everything his parents did annoyed him. He couldn't explain it.

"It's nothing," Howard said. "I just get bored."

"You'd rather play with that remote-controlled helicopter of yours," said his dad. His eyes narrowed.

"It's called a drone, Dad," said Howard, rolling his eyes. "You know that. You were there when I bought it."

This was Howard's sore spot, and his dad knew it. He brought it up any time he was trying to win a fight. The drone wasn't just a hobby to Howard. It was a way of life.

"And I never would have allowed it if I knew it would get in the way of your studies."

"Get in the way? I have all As. I always have all As," said Howard. He stood up from the table and brought his bowl over to the sink. "School bores me out of my mind. They dumb everything down!"

Howard dumped the remainder of his cereal into the stainless steel sink. He mashed the soggy flakes down into the garbage disposal. Down and out of sight. He didn't bother to turn the disposal on, though.

"You're sixteen," said his dad. "You go to school. Every day. I don't care how above it you think you are. Those are the rules. And when you're an adult, guess what? You'll go to work every day. That's life."

"That's your life," said Howard under his breath.

He didn't dare say it at full volume. He was angry, he was annoyed, but he still respected his father. His dad worked hard to ensure Howard had a place in private school. Howard's family was all about work ethic. His grandfather had worked hard in some dirty factory when he came to California from Vietnam, saving so his father could go to college. Howard's father had inherited that trait, often working holidays and weekends to pay for Howard's schooling. He made sure they had a nice house in the suburbs, a car that matched everyone else's, food on the table, and clothes in the closet.

Howard understood all of that, but he was not his father, and he was most certainly not his grandfather. He wanted something else, something he couldn't quite put into words. But whatever it was, he knew he was tired of waiting for it.

CHAPTER 3

WHIRS AND CLICKS

Angelica Ramone closed her eyes, leaned back against the headrest, and gently massaged the bridge of her nose with her index finger. She had a headache but had taken her last aspirin a few hours ago. At least the back of the town car was cool and quiet. She could hear the noise outside, but it was muffled, removed. It reminded her of a television set through a shared wall in an apartment building.

Angelica thought back to her Brooklyn apartment from college. She thought about the loud neighbor who would laugh at TV shows so hard his laughter could be heard through the wall. She had been annoyed at first, but when he'd moved out, when his laughter had stopped, she had kind of missed him.

She missed everything about that apartment now. She missed going outside for a jog. She missed walking to the grocery store, even if the trek was uphill. Most of all, she missed sitting in a café with a cup of coffee and a good book.

But Brooklyn was a long time ago. This was Los Angeles. This was her current life, and she couldn't hide in the back of a car for the rest of it. Even if she wasn't anywere near close to ready to open the car door and face what was outside.

Angelica sighed and put on sunglasses with large, dark lenses that nearly covered her entire face. She unlocked the door and stepped out. The sun hit her first, but the camera flashes were a close second. Although why they'd need a flash on a day like today was beyond her.

It was sunnier than usual, and that was saying something. L.A. was always sunny. A few dozen photographers clustered outside her hotel. Ever since her breakup with Bradley Wilt, they'd been out in full force. But Angelica blamed herself for that. This is what she got for dating a co-star.

"Angelica! Over here!" a familiar voice called. It was the paparazzo with the George Lucas beard. Angelica recognized him right away. He was always there.

Next to him stood his friend, the woman who always shouted to her in both English and Spanish. "Angelica!" the photog yelled, followed by a sentence in Spanish.

Angelica didn't understand a word of it. She'd taken French in high school, and she wasn't even good at that language. She wasn't about to look either way, though. Not today.

Posing for a photo was the last thing on Angelica's mind. She just wanted to get inside, take something for her headache, and collapse on the oversized California king in her suite.

She'd been living at the hotel for two weeks now and had put no real effort into looking for a permanent residence. The hassle with the paparazzi was annoying, but she couldn't bring herself to think about relocating, let alone hire movers.

Despite what the army of photographers thought, Angelica was a person. She wasn't an object. She wasn't a robot who played make believe in hit film after hit film. She had just as many thoughts, opinions, and feelings as anyone else. She would deal with her breakup on her own terms and at her own pace.

As Angelica approached the hotel, the bellhop opened the door, smiling his usual nervous smile. Angelica always found it cute that he was so kind. Every time he was working, he tried his best to accommodate her, despite the nonsense outside.

She patted him on the shoulder as she walked by, breathing in the cold hotel air. In a few seconds, she'd be safe. She'd be alone in her room.

The bellhop hurried behind her as she walked to the elevator. He placed his key in the special slot below the row of buttons, then pressed the special suite button, marked *SU1*.

Angelica leaned her head back against the smooth, mirrored wall as the elevator climbed to the very top floor. The doors of the evalator opened, not onto a hallway, but directly into Angelica's room.

She stepped off and handed a folded-up fifty-dollar bill to the bellhop. The young man promptly rejected it with a wave of his hand.

"No, ma'am," he said. "That's too much. It's an honor enough to —"

"No," Angelica cut him off. "Take it. It's the least I can do."

The bellhop took the bill without looking at it and shoved it into his pocket. He seemed more than a little embarrassed.

"Th-thank you," he said, almost under his breath.

Angelica walked into her foyer as the elevator closed behind her. She popped one shoe off, then the other. She was happy to be rid of the high heels. She hadn't even noticed that her feet were hurting until this very moment.

In the large bathroom she found her aspirin and took two. Then she walked into her bedroom.

The room was a little cold, so she made her way to the balcony's sliding door and pulled it open. The warm breeze hit her.

Angelica took five steps and then collapsed on the bed. Finally, she was alone. She could drop her guard. She could have . . . the thought entered her mind like a bolt of lightning. It was in the freezer! She'd completely forgotten about it.

With a burst of energy, Angelica made a beeline to her suite's living room and adjoining full kitchen. She opened the freezer, and there it was: double-fudge brownie ice cream with that amazing chocolate swirl. Becky had come through again.

Angelica had once cringed at the idea of hiring a personal assistant, but Becky had been a godsend. And acquiring a particularly hard-to-find ice cream seemed to be her specialty.

Pint in one hand, spoon in the other, Angelica made her way back to her bed. She hit the button on the TV remote on the nightstand and popped the ice cream's lid. Then she dug in, shoveling the ice cream to her mouth in enormous spoonfuls. She couldn't remember the last time she'd eaten anything this quickly.

The TV was loud. Louder than Angelica intended, but she couldn't be bothered to turn it down. She didn't share a wall with anyone these days, and she was exhausted. It was some type of nature show. A wolf was howling at the moon.

The sound filled her suite, so loudly that Angelica didn't even notice the whir and clicks from the drone outside her balcony window.

CHAPTER 4

UNDER THE BED

Howard trudged up to his room. He thought about slamming his door, but instead, he simply shut it quietly. Then he knelt down beside his bed and pulled out a large, custom control panel.

Howard had modified an old video game controller from the 1980s — the kind with a black joystick with a ball on the end — and improved it using spare parts from some of the computer mods he'd been messing with on the weekends.

The end result was a panel about the size of a board game box, with dials and switches, all with a retro look. It was like something from an airplane cockpit in an older movie. Or at least the arcade version of one.

One by one, Howard flipped a series of switches. In the corner of his room, his computer powered on. In another corner, his speakers whined to life.

Once everything was up and running, Howard plugged a black headset into the side of his control panel. A familiar voice sounded in his ear.

"About time you joined us, HowTo." It was the perky, optimistic voice of ParkourSisters.

That wasn't Parker Reading's real name, of course, just her screen name. It fit her. A pun within a pun. A tough name for a tough girl. But it was a goofy kind of tough, like her sense of humor.

"It's almost like you — gasp — went to school today!" said another voice.

This one was feminine as well but much more sarcastic. It belonged to Zor_elle — Zora Michaels in real life — the other female member of their online group.

Zora lived in Indiana — halfway across the country — and was probably Howard's closest friend. No . . . that wasn't quite right. She was the person in the group who shared the most of his interests.

Howard was into all things fantasy. Anything from movies starring trolls and elves, to role-playing games featuring wizards and warlocks, to comic books, Zora's main interest.

"I put in my hours," said Howard. "Sai here too?"

"If you'd check your monitor once in a while, you'd know the answer to that question is no," Zora said.

"Hey, I don't mock the beauty salon you call a bedroom, you don't mock my retro gaming style," Howard said.

"I should have never let you Skype with me," Zora said.

Howard fought back a grin. He could practically hear Zora rolling her eyes.

"Hey, you Skype with HowTo?" said Parker. "What about me?"

"I'm never home when you send me a request," said Zora.

"Well, perfect timing because I'm sending you one right now," said Parker. The humor was clear in her voice.

"Oops," Zora said quickly. "I think I hear my dad calling. Time for dinner. Talk to you guys tomorrow!"

There was a beeping sound in Howard's ear signaling Zora had disconnected. Lately it seemed harder and harder to get everyone online at the same time. But that's what happened when your team was spread out across the entire country.

Howard To, Parker Reading, Zora Michaels, and Sai Patel had never met in person, but they were more than just Internet friends. Sure, they'd all met on a message board originally, but their friendship had blossomed when they'd discovered a shared interest. They were all drone pilots with their own remote-operated UAVs — Unmanned Aerial Vehicles.

With Sai's design expertise to help them, they had formed their own secret message board. But more than that, they had formed their own community.

They'd decided to call their group SWARM, short for the Society for Web-Operated Aerial Remote Missions. They would use their love of drones to help other people, they decided.

They would take their hobby and do something good with it.

Although they'd had a few bumps in the road getting started, SWARM was now stronger than ever. It was a tight-knit group of four, and Howard had never known a support system quite like it — even if they weren't always working on the same case.

Parker started talking again. "It's because she's a girly girl," she said. "She thinks I'm gonna judge her."

"That's because you *will* judge her," said Howard. Now that they were alone on the line, he felt more at ease. He wasn't sure why that was.

"Fair point," said Parker. There was laughter in her voice. "So what's happening at the To household?"

"Just the usual parental lectures laced with disappointment," said Howard. "What's up in the big city?"

"Oh, you know. New York is still New York. One of the kids at my school fell in the subway tracks," she said. "But I helped pull him out with this other guy."

"Whoa!" said Howard. "That's crazy."

"Don't sound too impressed," said Parker. "It really wasn't that big a deal. There's always someone messing around on the platform. And there wasn't a train in sight."

"So who's this other guy? Your superhero partner?"

"I love this sound," said Parker.

"What?" Howard asked, confused.

"The sound of Howard To getting jealous. It's like my favorite thing in the world."

"I am not jealous," said Howard, rolling his eyes, even though he knew Parker couldn't see him. "Just curious about this guy you're hanging out with."

"Hey, speaking of red-hot love —"

"Wait, what red-hot —"

"Your girlfriend made the news today," Parker said.

"My girlfriend?"

"Angelica Ramone."

"Ooooh . . ." said Howard, finally getting the joke. "*That* girlfriend."

"You have so many," Parker quipped. "It must be hard to keep track."

"It's a curse, really," said Howard, smiling. "So what were you saying about Angelica? What happened?"

"Check your screen," Parker said. "It looks like she's not taking her recent breakup very well."

Howard stood up, tucking his control panel under one arm. He walked over to his desk to look at his state-of-the-art flat-screen computer monitor. On the screen, a pop-up window waited for him.

Using the track pad on his control panel, he clicked on the little window. It expanded and opened an instant message window with ParkourSisters. There was a photo attached to the message.

Howard opened the attachment, and there, in the attached photo, was Angelica Ramone, looking as amazing as ever. Beautiful big eyes, her trademark full bottom lip, blond hair falling to her shoulders. She was sitting on a white comforter in an expensive-looking hotel room and furiously eating a pint of chocolate ice cream.

At first Howard smiled, appreciating this rare glimpse into Angelica's private life. He usually wasn't big on celebrities, but there was something special about Angelica. Despite their more than ten-year age difference, he'd had a crush on her for the better part of a decade. He'd even felt a strange rush of hope when he heard she'd broken up with her longtime boyfriend.

Every time he traveled into L.A. from his suburb, Howard hoped he'd see her walking down the street or into some fancy restaurant. He knew it was a long shot, but it didn't stop him from hoping.

"Huh," Howard said into his headset. "How did they get such a . . . this isn't from a photo shoot."

"What do you mean?" asked Parker. "How do you know that?"

"This looks like it was taken at that fancy hotel, the Carmichael. She's staying there," he said.

"Um, stalk much?"

"Seriously," Howard said, "how did the paparazzi get this shot?"

Parker didn't say anything for a second. "You don't think . . ." she finally spoke.

"Yeah," said Howard. "I do."

"Bird in the air?"

"Already on it," said Howard.

He pressed a button on his control panel. It was red, the most noticeable button on the device. There was even text meticulously printed on the button. In capital letters, it read *LAUNCH*.

CHAPTER 5

OUT OF THE DOGHOUSE

There was a doghouse behind Howard To's house. The strange thing was, the To family had never actually owned a dog. The structure had come with the house when they'd bought it nearly ten years ago. The previous owners had managed to take their swing set with them — a heavy blow to six-year-old Howard at the time — but had left the doghouse in all its faded green glory.

It was the lone structure in an overgrown backyard that had taken the To family three years to get in order. No one gave it much thought aside from Howard.

When he was little, he'd been able to fit inside. It had served as his playhouse of sorts. By third grade, it had become his soccer goal. Its small opening had been a challenging target.

Now, the doghouse served its greatest purpose yet. It was home to Howard's "pet." It was the launching pad for his drone.

When Howard pressed the *LAUNCH* button on his control panel, the drone came to life. The dust and dirt on the ground scattered to the doghouse's interior walls, as though they were rushing to take cover from unexpected danger.

In the center of the house, resting in its charger base, was the red drone, its four black blades spinning feverishly. Soon the whirring rotors created enough lift to raise the craft off its base. It moved forward, following a carefully plotted course Howard had programmed more than a year ago.

The shiny red plastic glistened in the bright California sunshine as it escaped from the shade of the doghouse. As the machine rose up into the air, the red-and-yellow flame decals on each side of the main body became apparent.

The drone, which Howard had named the Redbird, was in no way a modest aircraft. It was the race car of SWARM and the boldest side of Howard's personality.

Sure, it was efficient with its small camera and sleek design. But the Redbird wanted the world to know it was there. It hummed almost silently in flight, but visually, it was as loud as drones came.

"Redbird is up," said Howard into his headset.

"Can you patch me in?" said Parker.

"Yes, ma'am," said Howard, pushing a few buttons on his control panel.

"Nope," Parker replied.

"What, the feed isn't working?" Howard asked. "I can see it on my end."

"The feed is fine. That's a nope to the ma'am talk," said Parker. "I'm like a half year younger than you."

Howard smiled. "Gotcha, Grandma," he said.

"You can't tell, but I'm kicking you over the Internet," said Parker.

Howard didn't answer. He was too busy typing something into the keyboard section of his control panel.

Finally, he said, "OK. I'm setting a course to the Carmichael now."

"Look at you, out to play white knight to your damsel in distress," said Parker, her tone teasing.

"Now who's jealous?" Howard said.

"I don't know," Parker replied. "Is that a trick question?"

CHAPTER 6

CRASHING DOWN

"Of course I didn't plan it, Jacob," Angelica Ramone snapped at the man across the table from her. He didn't seem to be paying attention to her, despite her serious tone.

"OK, then walk me through it," Jacob replied. He was shorter than Angelica, but sitting at the rooftop café, they looked equal in height.

"There's nothing to walk through," Angelica said. "Someone invaded my personal space.

They took a picture of me inside my hotel room."

"So they were out on your balcony?" Jacob said. He took a sip from his coffee. Part of the creamy drink stuck to his upper lip, giving him a makeshift mustache. He wiped it with a napkin, much to Angelica's relief.

"I don't know," Angelica said. "I don't know how they'd get up to the top floor. The Carmichael is the tallest building in that section of town."

"So we're talking about a telescopic lens from a nearby building?"

"I said I don't know." Angelica sounded more agitated now. "All I know is that it's an invasion of my privacy. I was on my bed."

"I know, I saw the photo."

"*Everyone* saw the photo. Didn't you read the papers? 'Depressed Angelica Eats Away Her Sorrows' — the tabloids had a field day with it."

"I don't know what you want me to do here," Jacob replied, shaking his head.

"You're my lawyer, Jacob," she said. "Just . . . just do *something*."

Jacob didn't respond. The photo was out there. There was nothing they could do at this point. Anything posted on the Internet was permanent. There was no getting around it, especially for a celebrity like Angelica.

Angelica sipped her coffee while Jacob thought things through. At least they were alone on the rooftop. Sure, there were paparazzi outside. They'd started gathering as soon as word spread that she was meeting her lawyer here for coffee. But this rooftop seating was reserved for Hollywood's A-list. Which was probably why Angelica liked it so much. No one would bother her up here.

Angelica's thoughts drifted to her ex, Bradley. And then to Sammy, the German shepherd puppy he'd adopted a month ago. If she was honest with herself, she missed the dog more than the boyfriend. At least Sammy had been a good listener.

It hit her all at once. The heartbreak. The never-ending public scrutiny. Sammy. It all seemed to come crashing down on her. Before she even realized what she was doing, Angelica had her face in her hands, crying.

The whole thing seemed to take Jacob by surprise. He didn't know exactly what to do. He certainly didn't know what to say. He just froze in place. He looked like a statue.

Angelica took off her sunglasses. She wiped her eyes with her fingers. "Do you have a tissue?" she asked. She was instantly embarrassed by how weak her voice sounded.

"Oh, yes, yes," said Jacob. He popped open his briefcase, reached inside, and pulled out a pack of tissues. He might not be much use in an emergency, but at least he came prepared for one.

Angelica took a tissue and blew into it. She almost looked like a cartoon character blowing into a cloth handkerchief. Then she looked up, and Jacob cringed despite himself.

"What?" she said.

He reached into his briefcase and handed her another tissue. "You've got a little . . ." He trailed off, not wanting to finish his own sentence.

Angelica covered her face. Her cheeks turned a shade of bright red. She snatched the tissue from Jacob and wiped the disgusting display from under her nose. She couldn't remember the last time she had felt this embarrassed. Wait, yes she could. It was when that unflattering picture of her eating ice cream in bed had surfaced on the Internet the night before. At least no one besides Jacob was here to see her . . .

Click.

This time Angelica heard it. It was quiet up on the café's rooftop. There was no loud television to drown out the sound.

She looked up from the table to see a black drone with a camera lens in its center hovering in the air. The lens was focusing on her, clicking rapidly now.

Angelica's mouth fell open. The drone had seen everything. Her blowing her nose like a child. Her crying like a schoolgirl dumped by her prom date. All her raw, private emotions captured for everyone to see. This was how they'd caught her in her hotel room. It was all the fault of this evil jet-black machine.

Jacob was blissfully unaware of the whole situation. He had no idea why Angelica started shouting. He didn't know why she stood up and quickly positioned her dark sunglasses over her eyes. And he didn't understand why she stormed off the rooftop, down the stairs to the café, and out onto the street below.

"Miss Ramone!" a man shouted from the sidewalk. He was right next to Angelica, but he was shouting anyway.

"Angelica!" said another man. "How does it feel to be single again?"

Angelica didn't answer. The crowd outside the café flashed their cameras and screamed their questions. They followed her as she made her way to her car and kept pace with her as she backed out of her parking space, nearly hitting the woman with the too-large camera. And they even jogged after her as she drove away.

CHAPTER 7

THE FIRST MEETING

"There it is!" Howard shouted into his headset.

"Come on, man," said Parker. "You trying to make me go deaf?"

"Look," said Howard, pointing at his computer monitor in his bedroom. It took him a second to realize that Parker couldn't see him. She was on the other side of the country, in New York City. Even though it felt like it at times, she was certainly not in the room with him.

"What exactly am I looking at?" Parker asked.

"I spotted another drone," Howard said. "It was fleeing the scene. How could you have missed it?"

"Do you want the honest answer?" Parker asked. Her voice was playful as usual. "I've been watching kung fu movies this whole time we've been talking."

"Hold on!" said Howard.

Even if Parker thought this was a joking matter, Howard was quite serious at the moment. He was working the controls on his large panel with total focus. This was intense, and it required every bit of Howard's concentration.

"Honestly, your whole celebrity crush thing is a little boring," Parker continued, knowing she'd be ignored. She was having fun with him now. She always had fun ruffling Howard's feathers.

Howard didn't answer. He was too busy piloting. The other drone was in his sights again. While he couldn't make out all the details, it was clear the thing was expensive. It had a large camera that Howard could even see from the back.

The Redbird swooped down, heading toward the restaurant. Then it buzzed the same rooftop as its prey and dove over the same striped awning.

The other drone was moving a bit slower than the Redbird for the time being. Howard thought he'd be able to catch up to it in another second or two.

"So . . . what's the endgame here?" asked Parker. "You going to try to knock that thing out of the sky? I'm no lawyer, but that's gotta be illegal."

"He's the one . . ." Howard said, trailing off as he forced the Redbird into another dive with the thrust of his joystick. "He's the one breaking the law."

"He was just flying over that restaurant," said Parker. "Who's he hurting?"

"He took pictures of Angelica in her hotel room!" Howard said. "He invaded her privacy! That's not right!" He had almost caught up to the black drone at this point. And better yet, it didn't seem to have noticed him.

"And you can prove that?" said Parker. "You know with absolute certainty that this is the same drone?"

"Well, not with *absolute* certainty, but —" Howard started.

Just then, the black drone spun around. It came to an abrupt stop in midair. The Redbird had been spotted.

"Watch out!" screamed Parker in Howard's ears. Now she was the one yelling.

Howard jolted back in his chair. He yanked up on his left joystick as hard as he could.

"Eeeayyyhhh!" That was as close as he could get to an actual word.

The Redbird obeyed his commands. It climbed up sharply, avoiding the hovering black drone by mere inches.

Howard regained his composure, as did the Redbird. He gradually slowed his drone's speed and circled it back around until he was facing the black drone once again — or at least he thought he was. But the other drone had disappeared.

"Where is it?" Parker was saying. "Where did it go?"

"I-I thought it was right there!" said Howard. "How long did it take me to turn around?"

"Long enough, I guess," Parker said. She sounded as frustrated as Howard felt.

Howard pointed the Redbird at the ground. There was an alley below, but there was no one in it. Next he moved the Redbird in a large circle, searching for any signs of movement.

"Is that it?" Parker said. Something dark had just disappeared over the neighboring building, and her voice was filled with excitement.

"Going to top speed," Howard said. He positioned his fingers on his control panel to do just that.

At Howard's command, the Redbird buzzed forward. The flames on its sides seemed appropriate as it swerved around a billboard and turned a corner.

Perched on the rooftop's ledge was the moving thing Parker had noticed on her screen. But now the thing was still. It seemed almost afraid. At the very least it was concerned, on edge.

It was not, however, the black drone. It was a pigeon.

"Yeah . . . so that's not the drone," said Parker.

"You think?" said Howard, his tone a little more annoyed than hers.

"I think you lost him," she said.

"*I* lost him, huh?" Howard said.

There was more kindness in his voice now. Parker had an impressive ability to make him smile, even in the most frustrating of circumstances.

"You only have yourself to blame," she said in her familiar sarcastic tone.

"I'm gonna do another sweep of the area before I head home to recharge," Howard said.

"Good idea," Parker agreed. "I'm gonna rewind my kung fu movie and see what parts I missed."

"You do that," Howard said. He smiled, but he made sure he didn't laugh. Parker didn't need any more encouragement.

The few paparazzi who had remained outside the café after Angelica's departure didn't pay any attention to the Man in Black as he made his was across the street. They were too busy making calls and trying to find out the next hot spot to push their cameras into someone's face. There was always a new location to get to.

If any of them had glanced at the Man in Black, perhaps they would have noticed his face. Perhaps they would have wondered what could have made this odd gentleman smile.

No one had gotten a photo of any importance. No one had taken a shot that would pay a significant amount of money or make the front cover of a magazine. By all accounts, it had been a bust.

But despite that bad luck, the man was smiling.

The Man in Black picked up his black drone from the sidewalk and placed it in his trunk. Then he got inside his dark car and drove away.

CHAPTER 8

CAUGHT IN THE ACT

"Really, Mr. To?" said Dr. Fletcher as he took the cell phone out of Howard's hands.

Howard didn't respond. He'd been too engrossed in the story he was reading to pay attention to his surroundings. Dr. Fletcher had stopped talking a few seconds ago. That should have been the first clue. The teacher had been droning on and on about hydrogen molecules, as if Howard needed a refresher on a subject he'd studied three years ago. It had seemed the perfect time for Howard to check his email on his phone.

Sure, cell phones were strictly prohibited in class, but Howard had propped his textbook at just the right angle. He'd been sure he'd disguised his actions well enough that Dr. Fletcher couldn't tell what he was doing. So he'd clicked the link Parker had emailed to him.

In retrospect, Howard hadn't given Dr. Fletcher enough credit. Perhaps he was sharper than some of the other teachers. He did have a doctorate, after all. Maybe he'd taken a course on how to spot slackers — or maybe Howard just wasn't as clever as he thought he was.

"Let's see here," said Dr. Fletcher, inspecting the smartphone in his hand. "Looks like Howard's got himself a crush — Angelica Ramone." The class began to snicker and giggle. "Well, I can't say you have bad taste."

The teacher walked up to the front of the class and put Howard's phone in his desk drawer. "You can have that back at the end of the day," said

Dr. Fletcher. "It'll come wrapped in a shiny new letter for your parents to sign."

That was the last thing Howard needed, but at least he was *at* school today. His parents couldn't get mad at him for skipping again.

Every day in this bland, boring building seemed like a waste to Howard. High school was not his thing. He had a few friends, sure, but *few* was the operative word. He really hadn't met anyone he clicked with outside of Drone Academy.

Howard smiled, despite his current situation. Drone Academy — Parker had made up that name. As if SWARM wasn't enough of a title. She had to add her spin to it. Her color commentary always made his day.

To be fair, Parker's nickname was somewhat accurate. SWARM *was* a school . . . of sorts. Howard wouldn't be half the pilot he was today without Parker's tips, or Zora's, or even Sai's.

They all helped each other with various missions, and Howard learned something every time.

Although he wasn't sure what the Angelica mission *was*, Parker was his partner. Whether he liked it or not. She'd had a point yesterday. If Howard was going to take down the black drone, he had to catch it doing something illegal.

Before his phone had been confiscated, Howard had had enough time to scan the article Parker had sent. It showed the most unflattering photos of Angelica that Howard had ever seen. She was crying at that café, covered in tears and snot and smeared makeup. It was a far different view than what the media normally showed. Angelica was usually so poised and perfect.

Seeing her human like that didn't lessen Howard's crush on her, however. It just made him want to help her even more.

He opened up his notebook and began to scribble down ideas for drone modifications. He'd been brainstorming since last night and figured he might as well draw up a rough sketch now. If he was lucky, he might even be able to start construction during study hall. He had some of the raw materials in his locker, and it wouldn't take too long.

Howard started drawing faster, looking up occasionally to make sure Dr. Fletcher wasn't watching. So far, so good.

Seventeen minutes later, the bell rang. Howard again looked up at Dr. Fletcher. The teacher was indeed watching Howard now, shaking his head.

Howard stacked his chemistry book on top of his notebook and made his way toward the door. He felt lighter without his phone in hand, which wasn't a good feeling. Howard was scrawny enough. Being lighter wasn't a good thing.

* * *

The elevator came to a smooth stop on the fifty-fifth floor. Angelica secured the brightly patterned scarf around her hair, adjusting it to cover her recognizable strands. The L.A. sun was brilliant as she stepped out onto the rooftop, even through the dark shade of her sunglasses.

Two men — a large man wearing dark sunglasses and a small man wearing regular eyeglasses — escorted her across the roof. The small man said something into his walkie-talkie as he trailed behind. Angelica couldn't quite make it out. The tall man was walking her forward, like she was the president. Like the safety of the country depended on Angelica making it across that rooftop.

Normally, Angelica found this sort of heightened security annoying. She always appreciated the work of bodyguards, but she hated restrictions to her freedom. But today, with the fresh memory of that black drone spying on her, she didn't mind the escort at all.

Less than a minute later, Angelica found herself being helped up into a helicopter. The chopper was silver and shiny, with the hotel's logo emblazoned across its side. It was almost enough to make her transfer hotels. The Carmichael was nice, but the private helipad at this particular establishment was certainly enticing.

The door of the helicopter closed, leaving Angelica alone with the pilot. The pilot, a young woman, turned around to smile at Angelica. She was younger than Angelica had expected. But there was a confidence in her eyes that said she knew what she was doing — or she was really good at faking it.

Either way, Angelica didn't feel a rush of adrenaline or fear when the helicopter rose off the fifty-fifth floor of the hotel. She looked out the window. No black drone in sight. No, as they took off, Angelica felt nothing but relief.

CHAPTER 9

TAKING THE SHOT

"He's here somewhere," Howard was saying.

"You're sure?" Parker asked through the headset. "Maybe this guy was just a fan and decided he had enough. He might even be a bigger fan than you are . . ."

Howard didn't appreciate the tone. Parker was kidding, but she seemed more serious than usual. She wasn't being playful. "Listen," he said, "if I could find her location just by checking a hotel employee's Facebook page, so could the other guy."

"The black knight," said Parker. "Good thing a white knight is here to save the lady's honor."

"Boy, you're fun today," said Howard. He didn't know what he'd done to make her mad, but Parker didn't seem in the mood for their mission. She seemed to disapprove of it entirely.

"I do what I can," said Parker. Her tone was light again. She seemed back to her old self.

Howard didn't have time to think about Parker's sudden change in attitude. He was on the hunt for the black drone.

"All right, there's the helicopter," he said. "And it's lifting off now . . ."

Howard had positioned the Redbird on the rooftop of the hotel's stairwell and was using its camera to scan the area. Despite the drone's bright coloring, he hoped it wouldn't be spotted. The last thing he wanted to do was make Angelica feel even more threatened. But so far, neither the security team nor Angelica seemed to have noticed Redbird. Howard could only hope the black drone wouldn't notice him either.

"Where are you?" Howard muttered.

"I'm sitting in my room downing an entire box of cheese crackers," came Parker's response. It wasn't the answer Howard was looking for, but it did make him smirk.

Then he spotted it. As the helicopter lifted off, the black drone rose into view from the side of the building. It began to follow the chopper.

"There it is," he said. "But what is he doing? No way he can keep up with her."

"No way you can, either," Parker said. "What's the plan again?"

"Watch and learn, grasshopper," said Howard.

"Have you been secretly paying attention to my kung fu movie recommendations?" asked Parker.

"Wouldn't you like to know," Howard quipped. "Now, I just gotta get close enough . . ."

The Redbird lifted off its perch and made a beeline for the black drone. With his control panel on his lap, Howard lifted a tiny new remote control from his pocket. It had a single black button in its center. He held the remote tightly in his right hand, steering the Redbird with his left, and studied his computer monitor. He steered the Redbird so that the black drone was framed directly in the center of his live feed.

But the black drone was quicker than the Redbird. Howard couldn't close the distance.

"I'm gonna have to take the shot," he said.

"What shot?" Parker asked.

Howard didn't answer. He'd spent all of study hall and an hour after school on the Redbird's modifications. His drone was now armed.

A suction-cup pistol, which Howard had owned for nearly a decade, was attached to the side of the Redbird. The gun was small, compact, and could only fire once without a manual reload, but it would have to do. Howard had also added a counterweight on the opposite side of the drone to balance it out and stabilize the vehicle. Then he'd modified the power directed to the Redbird's blades. They needed to spin faster than ever before.

But most of Howard's time that afternoon had been spent on the suction-cup projectile. His toy gun no longer shot its tiny red suction cup bullet — now it shot a tracking device.

It was really a GPS chip, a simple piece of technology easily purchased at an electronics store. Howard had bought his a while ago. He was always buying bits of tech here and there to tinker with. But it wasn't until today that he'd sprayed the chip with a fast-working epoxy. Now, if the GPS chip touched anything, it would adhere to it tighter than a magnet to a refrigerator.

All Howard had to do was fire his gun with the trigger he'd rigged up. That, and not miss.

That was the theory, at least. Howard hadn't had time to test it out.

"Target locked," Howard said, even though he didn't possess the kind of technology needed to lock onto anything. It was just something they said in the movies. He had the black drone in his sights.

Howard pressed the flat button on the remote in his right hand, squeezing it much tighter than necessary. "And . . . firing," he said.

With a rather anticlimactic click, the toy gun shot off. The GPS chip, on its plastic rubber base, shot out of the barrel and sped through the air.

Years of practice with the suction-cup gun paid off. Howard hit his target — and better yet, it stuck. The black drone was now flying with a GPS chip attached to its rear.

"Whoa!" said Parker. "You got it!"

"Uh-huh," Howard said, trying to sound confident. He hadn't felt that way, but he didn't want Parker to know that.

"Is that a —" Parker started to say.

"A GPS chip," Howard finished. "I've got his location now. Wherever he goes. I've got him."

Howard slowed the Redbird as the black drone peeled away through the sky. If he hadn't made that shot, there was no way Howard could have kept up. Whoever was piloting that drone had money and tech know-how. But now Howard had time. He could regroup and catch the black drone in the act.

"Way to go, white knight," Parker said in his ear. "You're on your way to a celebrity girlfriend after all."

She was trying to hide it, but her tone had shifted again. Howard wondered why.

CHAPTER 10

HIDE AND SEEK

Angelica looked over the railing of the bridge at her reflection below. The image was hazy, just a shadow of her form rippling along with the water of the creek.

She smiled. It was the first time she'd been out of focus for a while. It was nice. This trip had been a good idea after all.

The ranch was only a forty-five-minute helicopter ride from downtown Los Angeles. It wouldn't have taken that much longer by car, but Angelica couldn't risk the paparazzi following her. If the tabloids got wind of her visiting her old boyfriend, Jonathan Keaton, she'd never hear the end of it.

She and Jonathan were just friends now, but that wouldn't matter. There'd be endless gossip articles about rekindled flames. There'd be jokes on late-night talk shows. And worse, there would be even *more* photographers camped outside her hotel in the morning.

The simple truth was, Angelica needed someone to talk to. Jonathan had always been there for her. Right after the news broke of her split with Bradley, Jonathan had called to offer a friendly ear or a shoulder to cry on. There was nothing romantic about it. When she really thought about it, she realized that Jonathan was her best friend.

"Dinner is almost ready," Jonathan said as he walked out onto the small wooden bridge with her. He was wearing his cowboy hat. Angelica had only seen him wear it on the ranch. "Hope you like your steak well done."

"Not really," she said, smiling at the welcome company.

"Well, too bad," he said. "'Cause I overcooked 'em."

"Yet again."

"One of these days I'll learn to pay attention when I've got meat on the grill," he said. "But the Lakers game was on. It was out of my hands."

Angelica put her arm through Jonathan's as he walked her down the path and onto his well-manicured lawn, and leaned her head on his shoulder. This man was like a brother to her. He was family. But yet, the paparazzi would see it another way. She had to hide their friendship for the sake of her own sanity.

"I want to thank you again for —" Angelica stopped talking as soon as she heard it. It was that familiar *whir* and *click*. Just like on the rooftop café. They had found her again. *It* had found her.

Angelica spun around to see the black drone above her. It was hovering in the air, staring at her with its one glass eye. The clicking was rapid now. It didn't want to miss any of what surely was Angelica's new "love affair."

When Jonathan noticed Angelica had turned, he did the same. He looked up at the drone, feeling Angelica release his arm. "What is that . . . wait, is that a drone?"

"It's been following me all week," Angelica said, turning away and covering her face with her hands in a sudden burst of panic. "We need to get inside — now!"

"Wait," said Jonathan. "What about that?"

Angelica turned to look in the direction her friend was pointing. "What?" she said.

"Now there's two of 'em," Jonathan said.

CHAPTER 11

THE END OF THE WAITING PERIOD

"I can't believe this GPS tracker cost you thirty bucks," Parker said through the headset.

"Thirty-three ninety-nine" said Howard. "Worth every penny." He was concentrating on piloting, but there was always time for a little banter. They had been following the GPS signal for the better part of an hour, and only now did the black drone seem to be slowing down.

"Any idea where you are?" Parker asked.

"Some sort of ranch," said Howard. "Must belong to one of Angelica's friends or something."

"I can see the UAV on screen," said Parker as Howard's drone drew closer to the GPS signal. The black drone was right where the tracker had said it would be. The plan was going like clockwork.

"Uh-huh," said Howard.

"So now we just observe," said Parker. "Right? We sit and wait and catch it in the act?"

"Uh-huh," Howard said again.

"I only ask because you seem to be picking up speed."

"Uh-huh."

"Howard!" said Parker. Her voice was excited now. "This is totally not the plan!"

"No," said Howard. He pulled back on the joystick on his control panel as hard as he could, picking up even more speed. He was surprised it didn't snap off. "No, it is not."

"Ooooh no," Parker said under her breath.

Howard didn't reply. He had officially run out of patience.

Everything in his life was a waiting game. High school. He had to wait out the boring classes until he could finally challenge himself in college.

Money. He couldn't afford the equipment the black drone's owner indulged in. Howard was just in high school, after all. He was usually broke and wouldn't have that kind of income for a decade or so, after he landed a real job.

Girls. He had to wait that out too. Wait for them to notice him. Wait for his youthful quirks to mature into interesting qualities. He'd never had a real connection with any girl he could think of. But while he wouldn't admit it, Howard had a tendency to miss the obvious.

Angelica was different, though. She seemed down to earth. She seemed secure in who she was, not someone looking for attention at every moment. And now Angelica was being stalked, and all he could do was just wait it out. But no, there was one other option.

So that day, as Angelica and her friend hurried to get out of sight, Howard decided to stop waiting. He pointed the Redbird straight toward the unsuspecting black drone. Before Parker could stop him or he could second-guess himself, Howard rammed his drone straight into the other one.

It felt good. When both drones came crashing down to the grass below, Howard felt satisfied.

That is, until Parker spoke. "Well, that was certainly something," she said.

Howard was smiling when he answered. "That will end that," he said. But his grin only lasted another fifteen seconds. Because after that, the black drone began to move again.

Howard could see it clearly in his camera. The black drone's front blades moved first. It was just a twitch or two initially, but soon they were spinning at top speed, as were the back two blades. Before Howard could let out a word, the black drone was in the air again.

The same couldn't be said for the Redbird. It was completely dead. The collision had totaled three of its four blades, according to the readout on Howard's monitor.

All he could do was sit and watch the black drone follow Angelica and her friend. It trailed behind them until they were all out of view.

Howard tried to adjust his camera angle, but the camera wasn't working, either. "That couldn't have gone worse," he finally said.

"Oh," said Parker into his ear. "Sure it could've."

CHAPTER 12

NOTES FROM THE
RIDE-ALONG

Howard couldn't seem to stop staring at his computer screen. He was completely speechless.

It had been a week since he and Parker had spoken. Howard had taken some time away from SWARM. Time to mourn the loss of the Redbird and to plan out his next steps.

But even now, a week later, he couldn't find the right words to say. All he could come up with was: "Are you serious? Are you even serious right now?"

"Technically those two questions are the same question," said Parker. Her voice was lighthearted, but her trademark sarcasm was still there.

"How did you even . . . when did you think to do this?"

"I wasn't the pilot," Parker explained. "I was just the ride-along. While you were busy playing drone chicken, I was busy clicking away."

"I just . . . can't get over this," Howard said. "Won't they know where they came from and trace them back to you?"

"I submitted the pictures as an anonymous tip," Parker said.

On Howard's screen was a newspaper article — not from a trashy gossip magazine but from a legitimate L.A. paper. The headline read, "Drone Pilot Arrested on Trespassing Charges."

On the cover of the paper was a man dressed in black and white. He had black glasses and flawless, slicked-back hair.

"So you took pictures," Howard said. "The whole time I was piloting the drone, you were snapping photos."

"Yep," said Parker. "Well, screen shots. The Redbird was doing all the filming. I was just capturing everything for posterity."

"And you sent them to the press? Shots of the black drone invading Angelica's privacy? Shots of the Redbird fight?"

"All of it," Parker replied. "With a lengthy explanation. I even sent them your address, just in case Angelica Ramone wants to send you back your totaled drone."

"Wow," said Howard.

"I know, right?" said Parker. "Am I an awesome friend or what? I wouldn't even be surprised if Angelica herself calls you up some time to personally thank you. You might get that dream date after all. You can thank me later."

"About that . . ." Howard said, taking a deep breath. "I think I was kind of . . . I mean, I thought about all the stuff you said this week . . ."

For once, Parker was uncharacteristically silent.

"You were right," said Howard. "I *was* trying to help . . . but it was probably for the wrong reasons. I wanted to be some hero more than I wanted to stop the bad guy. Kinda messed up, huh?"

"Well . . ." Parker said slowly. "Yeah. That's a little messed up. But I'll let it slide. You are a teenage guy, and she's a movie star. It's all good."

"Yeah?"

"Yeah."

"Well, thanks," Howard said. He paused, thinking for a moment how much Parker seemed to get him, then changed the subject. "So I've been meaning to tell you, I got a job this week while I was taking some time off from SWARM."

"Oh, yeah?"

"It's at this local tech startup. No big deal or anything, but I get to fiddle with all sorts of stuff that's above my pay grade."

"Like paper and glue?"

"Ha!" Howard laughed. "Yeah, just like that. But either way, I'll finally have something to keep me busy, you know? Challenge me a little bit."

"Sounds like you can finally save up some money and come visit me here in New York," Parker said.

Howard was grinning without realizing it — blushing a little too. "Now why would I do that?" he asked.

"Someone needs to rescue me from another summer spent locked in my poorly air-conditioned apartment, listening to the neighbors argue."

"I can do that," said Howard.

"Of course you can," said Parker. "You're my white knight."

"Takes one to know one," Howard said.

With that, Parker clicked out of the conversation, leaving Howard alone in his room.

He stood up, stretched his arms over his head, and walked out through his door. It was time for dinner, and he saw no reason to wait until he was called.

CHAPTER 13

NO REASON TO SMILE

The Man in Black didn't like the music in the elevator. It was instrumental, like his beloved classical music, but it was modern. Some eighties song he couldn't quite put his finger on. All he knew was that it was awful. It wasn't soothing in the slightest.

When the doors opened, the large police officer ushered him out into the hall. The Man in Black walked through the precinct. No eyes were on him. That didn't bother him at first. It was his job to put the public's eyes on someone else. The more they looked, the more money he made.

Everyone else in the precinct was standing near the corner. It struck the Man in Black as odd . . . until he saw the person they were gathered around.

It was Angelica Ramone, the woman who had made him a lot of money these past few days. Until now. Until she decided to press charges, and the police decided to take his drone. Now she was costing him money.

Angelica seemed to be telling some story to the officers. She was entertaining them, and they were obviously smitten with her. But when the Man in Black was paraded past her, Angelica paused. She locked eyes with the Man in Black. And then she smiled before going back to her story.

The Man in Black did not return the grin. He didn't part his lips and show off his immaculate white teeth. Instead, he looked at the ground. Unlike Angelica, he had no reason to smile.

ABOUT THE AUTHOR

The author of the Amazon best-selling hardcover *Batman: A Visual History*, Matthew K. Manning has contributed to many comic books, including *Beware the Batman, Spider-Man Unlimited, Pirates of the Caribbean: Six Sea Shanties, Justice League Adventures, Looney Tunes,* and *Scooby-Doo, Where Are You?* When not writing comics themselves, Manning often authors books about comics, as well as a series of young reader books starring Superman, Batman, and the Flash for Capstone. He currently resides in Asheville, North Carolina, with his wife, Dorothy, and their two daughters, Lillian and Gwendolyn. Visit him online at www.matthewkmanning.com.

GLOSSARY

adhere (ad-HEER) — to hold fast or stick by or as if by gluing, suction, grasping, or fusing

aerial (AIR-ee-uhl) — relating to aircraft

anonymous (uh-NON-uh-muhs) — of unknown authorship or origin

drone (drohn) — an aircraft or ship without a pilot that is controlled by radio signals

expoxy (ih-POK-see) — a synthetic resin used mostly in coatings and adhesives

immaculate (ih-MAK-yuh-lit) — spotlessly clean

legitimate (li-JIT-uh-mit) — conforming to recognized principles or accepted rules and standards

meticulous (muh-TIK-yuh-luhs) — extremely or overly careful in thinking about or dealing with small details

mortified (MAWR-tuh-fahyd) — greatly embarrassed or humiliated

paparazzi (pah-puh-RAHT-zee) — freelance photographers who aggressively pursue celebrities for the purpose of taking candid photographs

DISCUSSION QUESTIONS

1 Talk about the relationship Howard has with Zora compared to the relationship he has with Parker. How are they different?

2 Why do you think Parker seemed irritated with Howard during parts of their mission? Discuss some possible reasons.

3 Howard views Angelica as being different from other celebrities. Do you think that's a realistic expectation? Why or why not?

WRITING PROMPTS

1 Imagine you are a member of SWARM. Write a paragraph describing your drone. What would it look like, and what characteristics would it have?

2 Pretend you are Angelica and write a letter to Howard after the drone crash. What would you want to say to him?

3 Why do you think the Man in Black was so focused on Angelica? Was it his job or something more? Write a paragraph discussing the motivation behind his actions.

READ ALL THE OTHER

DRONE ACADEMY

MISSIONS

Despite being a founding member of Drone Academy, **Zora Michaels** is viewed as a flighty girly-girl by her fellow high schoolers. Little do they know, Zora's real passion lies behind her keyboard. But when the younger brother of a classmate goes missing, during a forest fire no less, it's up to Zora to use her drone to locate and rescue the runaway, all while keeping her identity a secret from her increasingly nosy peers.

When **Parker Reading** learns that a local bank robber has eluded authorities in her hometown, she begins to hunt him down, using her computer skills and sleek drone to scan the streets of her city. But when the thief turns the tables, Parker goes from being in virtual danger to real-life jeopardy.

Sai Patel takes every opportunity to stand up for underdogs being cyber-bullied. But Sai's life takes a dramatic turn when a nemesis customizes a drone to look exactly like Sai's, using it to commit theft, interrupt emergency rescues, and cause as much trouble as possible. Now Sai must prove his innocence using his own drone to bring its doppelgänger to justice.

9